Running
SCARED

TEXT BY EMMA CARLSON BERNE
ILLUSTRATED BY KATIE WOOD

raintree 🍃

a Capstone company — publishers for children

Raintree is an imprint of Capstone Global Library Limited, a company
incorporated in England and Wales having its registered office at 264
Banbury Road, Oxford, OX2 7DY – Registered company number:
6695582

www.raintree.co.uk
myorders@raintree.co.uk

Graphic Designer: Kristi Carlson
Production Specialist: Laura Manthe
Illustrated by Katie Wood
Originated by Capstone Global Library Ltd
Printed and bound in China

ISBN 978 1 4747 3228 4
20 19 18 17 16
10 9 8 7 6 5 4 3 2 1

British
A full ⟨   ⟩ Library.

Every ⟨   ⟩ erial
reprod   equent
printin

CONTENTS

Chapter one

WARMING UP

"Come on, Liv!" someone shouted.

Olivia looked out the window and saw her best friend Jessica waiting for her. Jessica had her foot propped against a tree as she stretched.

"I'm going running with Jessica," Olivia called to her mother. She tied her running shoes and hurried out the door.

"Hey," she said, smiling at Jessica. "How's your knee?"

Jessica had pulled a tendon on the side of her knee a couple weeks ago. This was the first time they'd gone running together since the injury.

Jessica bent forwards and reached her fingers towards her foot. "It's a lot better," she said. "I think I should be good for the track team trials next week. How about you?"

Olivia nodded but didn't say anything. Jessica had been talking about joining the track team lately, but Olivia wasn't so sure about it.

The girls finished stretching and set off running. They both stuck to the side of the street. Running on the concrete pavement was really hard on their joints. Asphalt was much better.

"Make sure to start slow," Jessica said. "We have to pace ourselves if we want to do five kilometres."

"I know," Olivia agreed. "I always want to start out so fast."

The two girls ran without talking for a few minutes. Olivia let her mind empty out, like she usually did when she was running. She felt the steady pounding of her feet on the solid road. Her breathing was deep, but even. She could feel her heart beating steadily.

Up ahead, Olivia saw a long, steep hill. She glanced over at Jessica. "Ready for it?" she asked.

Jessica nodded. "Let's do it," she replied. The two friends high-fived and started the climb.

The sun was warm on their backs as they ran up the long hill. Olivia felt her leg muscles working to push her up the steep slope. She pumped her arms smoothly at her sides and kept her breathing steady, pacing herself.

Finally they reached the top of the hill. Olivia and Jessica stopped to rest, bending over with their hands on their knees. They were both breathing heavily.

"Whew!" Jessica said. She swiped her hand across her sweaty forehead. "I hope the track team practices aren't as hard as that hill. I'm exhausted!"

"So, are you serious about joining the team?" Olivia asked. She walked in a circle with her hands behind her head, trying to catch her breath.

"Definitely," Jessica said. "It's going to be great. You should do it, too."

"I don't know," Olivia said. "I'm more into running for the fun of it. Competing isn't really for me."

Jessica gave her a pleading look. "Please! You have to do it! It would be so fun!" she insisted. "We could lift share to practice and train together. It'll be just like what we do now. Plus, you're an awesome runner."

Olivia laughed. Jessica made it sound easy. "You're so impossible! I can't believe I'm even thinking about this," she said.

"Yes!" Jessica cheered. She grabbed Olivia's hand. "Does this mean you'll do it? Say yes!"

Olivia hesitated. *Oh, why not?* she thought. *It could be fun.*

"Okay, fine," she said. "I'll try out. But that doesn't mean I'll make it. I probably won't. I told you, I'm not good at actual competitions."

Jessica didn't even seem to hear her. She was too busy jumping up and down and clapping. "Yay!" she hollered. "This is going to be great!"

Olivia smiled. She hoped Jessica was right.

Chapter two

JUST PRACTICE

A week later, Olivia sat on the school's athletics field with the rest of the track team. Everyone was waiting to find out what events they would be running.

Olivia's stomach was in knots. The trials had been two days ago. Olivia had been so sure she wouldn't make the team that she hadn't even been nervous. But she had made it. That's when she started feeling anxious.

Please let me get a short distance, Olivia thought as she waited to hear the coach announce the events. She ran longer distances with Jessica, so she knew she could do it, but the idea of running in an actual race scared her.

Maybe I'll get lucky and get the 100 metre, Olivia thought hopefully. *At least with a sprint the race will be over faster.*

Mr Roberts started calling out names and distances. Everyone's faces lit up as they heard their names. The runners on the relay teams high-fived each other.

"Jessica Green, 400 metres," the coach called out.

"Yes!" Jessica exclaimed, grinning. Olivia wasn't surprised. Her friend was a great sprinter. She just hoped she'd be as lucky.

"Olivia Pitman, 3200 metres," Mr Roberts continued.

Olivia's stomach sank. 3200 metres was the longest distance! She'd run that far with Jessica before, but this was different. People would be watching.

There's no way I'm going to be able to run that, she thought. *I'll just talk to Mr Roberts. He'll understand. Maybe he'll let me do a shorter distance.*

The other runners stood up and started gathering into groups based on their distances. Jessica hopped up and went to join the other sprinters.

Olivia gathered her courage and walked over to the coach. He was busy checking things off on his clipboard.

"Mr Roberts?" Olivia said hesitantly.

"Hi, Olivia," the coach said. He looked down and checked his clipboard again. "I have you down for 3200 metres. You distance runners should gather over by the long jump. Everyone's going to try out for their event." He hurried away before she had a chance to respond.

Olivia stood alone on the track. Not only was she stuck running the 3200, she was going to have to do it right now. Olivia willed herself not to cry as she went to join the other distance runners.

She didn't recognise any of the other kids on the track. *Everyone seems so excited,* Olivia thought miserably. *Except me.*

Across the track, Mr Roberts yelled, "Distance runners, please line up! Let's have you practise the 3200-metre race. That's eight laps."

The other runners spread out along the starting line. Olivia found herself in lane five. She crouched down in the starting position. One knee rested on the track while the other stretched out behind her. Her fingers were spread out and lightly resting on the ground.

Olivia could already feel her muscles getting tight. *It's just practice*, she told herself. *It doesn't even mean anything. Relax.* But her muscles wouldn't listen.

Mr Roberts held up his stopwatch. "And go!" he yelled.

The rest of the runners leapt off the starting line, but Olivia stumbled as she stepped forwards. She tried to get her balance back and pushed herself ahead. Around her, the others ran easily.

I have to keep up, Olivia thought anxiously. *I can't come in last at the first practice. It would be humiliating!*

Olivia's chest felt tight as her feet pounded the track. Her hands were clenched at her sides. *Breathe,* she thought. But the steady, even breathing she usually had when she ran was gone. Instead, she heard herself gasping for breath.

The other runners were starting to pull ahead of her now. Olivia started to panic. She forced herself to run faster until she was even with them. She could feel her form getting worse. Her arms were starting to flail at her sides.

"Relax, Olivia!" Mr Roberts called from the sidelines. "Keep your elbows by your side. Stay loose!"

Olivia barely heard her coach over her own ragged breathing. Somehow, she managed to finish the race. But as she staggered over the finish line in last place, she barely recognised herself.

Olivia gasped for breath. She'd never had this much trouble running before. What had happened to the girl who'd run five kilometres easily just last week?

Chapter three

FALLING APART

Olivia spent the rest of the practice watching the other runners train for their events. No one else seemed to have any trouble with their distances. Jessica did a great job. She came in first in her sprinting group.

Great, Olivia thought. *Now I look even worse. If I run this badly in practice, imagine what an actual race will be like. I can't do it. There's no way.*

Jessica came up to Olivia after practice. "What happened out there?" her friend asked. "We just went running, and you were totally fine. 3200 metres is only a few kilometres. You run more than that all the time."

"I don't know," Olivia replied. "I just panicked. I felt like everyone was watching, and I was going to come in last. Everything just fell apart."

"You're a great runner," Jessica said. "I doubt you would have come in last. You were probably just having an off day. I'm sure you'll do better next time."

"Yeah, maybe," Olivia agreed. She hoped Jessica was right, but privately she wasn't so sure.

Chapter four

FAKING IT

A week later, Olivia and Jessica sat on the sidelines near the track, stretching. The first meet of the season had already started.

Olivia stared at the runners warming up for the 800-metre race. The past two weeks of practice hadn't been bad. She'd completed the 3200 several times. But the moment she walked up to the track for the meet and saw the other competitors, her nerves came back.

Jessica noticed her friend's expression. "Relax!" she said. "You're going to be great. I don't know why you're so worried."

Olivia twisted her fingers together nervously as she watched the track. "Yeah. I'll be okay," she said. She couldn't bear to admit how scared she was.

"Oh, no! Look," Jessica said. She pointed down at the track below them.

The 800-metre race was almost half over. Most of the runners were running in a tight pack. But one of the runners was lagging way behind. His face was red, and he was clearly struggling. From up in the stands, Olivia could hear some other boys mocking the runner.

"He's so far behind," Olivia said. "I can't watch."

"I know," Jessica said. She shook her head. "It's awful. He must be so embarrassed."

The other runners crossed the finish line, and the blond boy was the only one left on the track.

Jessica's right, Olivia thought. *It's so embarrassing. What if that's me?*

The next few races passed in a blur. Then the announcer was calling the runners for the 3200. Olivia stood up and moved towards the starting line to take her place. She was in lane three, right in the middle.

The other runners found their lanes on both sides. *They all look so fast,* Olivia thought. She suddenly felt sick to her stomach. But before she could do anything, the starter raised his gun in the air.

"Mark!" he shouted.

The runners crouched down into position. Olivia pressed her fingers to the track. She felt as if every eye in the stands was glued to her.

"Set!" the starter called.

The runners tensed in anticipation. The starting gun cracked, and everyone shot from their crouches.

Too fast, Olivia thought right away. She shot a quick glance at the other runners. No one looked worried. Olivia tried to clear her mind and focus on keeping her breathing steady, like she did when she ran for fun. But all she could think about was whether she was fast enough.

I'll never be able to keep this up for the whole race! she thought.

Three laps down. The race wasn't even halfway over, and Olivia was already struggling to breathe. Her feet were so heavy. She felt herself dropping back. Two runners pulled ahead of her. Then three.

With four laps to go, Olivia dropped further back. There was only one more runner behind her. As they passed the stands, she heard Jessica call out, "You can do it, Liv!"

No, I can't! Olivia thought. The last runner was so close behind her that Olivia could hear the girl breathing. Slowly and steadily, the other girl pulled even with her and then ahead.

Olivia panicked. *I'm last!* she thought frantically. *Everyone is going to make fun of me!*

Then suddenly Olivia thought, *I won't do it. No. I can't!* She was nearing the end of the track. As she approached the stands again she slowed down abruptly. Olivia grabbed her leg and limped to a halt.

Even as she did it, Olivia knew it was wrong. But the fear of humiliation was too strong. She couldn't come in last – not with all these people watching.

Olivia limped off the track, still clutching her leg. The rest of the runners kept going. As Olivia stumbled to the sidelines, Mr Roberts hurried over to her. "What's wrong?" he asked.

"Leg cramp," Olivia said. She was lying, and it felt horrible. But at the same time, she was so relieved not to be in the race anymore.

Mr Roberts examined her leg, then straightened up and patted her on the shoulder. "Well, it happens to all of us sometimes," he said. "Why don't you sit down and try to stretch it out."

Olivia sat down and hid her face against her leg, pretending to stretch. But as she did it, she'd never felt so ashamed.

Chapter five

A PRIVATE PROMISE

The car park was full of cars as parents picked up their kids after the meet. Olivia spotted her mother's SUV in a corner. She walked towards it, trying to look happy.

"Hi, honey!" Mum said as Olivia climbed into the back seat. "I'm so sorry we couldn't see you run. I had a work meeting I couldn't get out of."

"That's okay," Olivia mumbled. "Don't worry about it."

Olivia's favourite aunt, Naomi, sat in the front passenger seat. She turned around, already smiling, as Olivia buckled her seatbelt. "How did the race go?" her aunt asked.

Olivia felt her face get hot as she thought about how she'd dropped out of the race. She swallowed hard. "Oh, just okay," she said, trying to sound casual.

"Why just okay?" Mum asked, pulling out of the crowded car park.

"Oh, um . . . my leg started to cramp up halfway through," Olivia told her. "I, uh, had to drop out."

Mum was concentrating on driving, but Aunt Naomi looked at her closely. Olivia stared out the window so she wouldn't have to meet her aunt's gaze.

"How'd you do before that?" Aunt Naomi asked.

"Fine," Olivia mumbled. She didn't trust herself to say anything more than that. She turned to stare out the window.

Aunt Naomi would never drop out of a race just because she was scared, Olivia thought. *If she finds out what I did she'll be so ashamed of me.*

As Mum turned the car into their driveway at home, Olivia made two private promises to herself. First, that Aunt Naomi would never find out what happened today. And second, that she would never drop out of a race again.

Chapter six

DISTANCE DROP OUT

Olivia stuck her legs out in front of her and leaned forwards. She felt the muscles along the backs of her legs stretch. Five days had passed since the last track meet.

Jessica sat down beside her. Her friend pulled her leg up towards her chest to stretch her hip muscles.

"This team doesn't look that fast," Jessica said. "It's going to be an easy meet, I can tell."

"I feel sick," Olivia said. She wasn't lying. Her stomach was rolling like she was about to throw up. But it wasn't because she'd eaten something bad or because she had the flu. Olivia felt sick because she knew she was going to do it again. She was going to drop out of the race.

It wasn't that she wanted to drop out of the race. In fact, what she really wanted to do was run. But as she looked around at the other team, she felt nervous. *What if I come in last?* Olivia thought. *Everyone will laugh at me.*

Jessica kept reading the meet schedule. "Oh, look, 3200 metres is up first," she said, pointing to the schedule.

As if on cue, a voice came over the loudspeaker. "3200 metres, first event," the announcer boomed.

Olivia took a deep breath and forced herself to stand up. As she walked past the stands, she heard Mum and Aunt Naomi yell, "Go, Olivia!"

Olivia swallowed hard. She couldn't look up at them. *Don't drop out,* she told herself. *Just run the race.*

Olivia took her place on the track in lane three. There were five other runners. One girl was almost two metres tall. *She's going to be fast,* Olivia thought nervously. *That means the pace is going to be really fast for everyone.*

Olivia crouched down at the starting line with the rest of the runners and positioned her feet in the starting blocks. She kept her left foot slightly ahead of her right, and rested her fingertips lightly on the ground.

Crack! The starter's gun sounded loudly. Olivia leapt off the line with the other runners. She had been right – the pace was fast. The tall girl sped to the front of the group. The others hurried to match the pace she set.

I can't do it! Olivia thought. *I can't come in last in front of Aunt Naomi.*

Olivia's breathing started to become ragged. Ahead of her, she could see the tall girl still leading the pack. Everyone else seemed to be running easily. They didn't seem to be struggling at all. The runners' long legs ate up the track.

Olivia glanced over to her right as the runners rounded the second bend. A dark-haired girl was running next to her. The girl's face was red, and she looked like she was struggling.

Maybe I can get ahead of her, Olivia thought. She concentrated on trying to pick up some speed so she could pass the other runner.

Suddenly the dark-haired girl shot her a glance and sped up, too. The girl pulled ahead of Olivia.

Olivia started to panic, just like she'd done in the last race. *There are still six more laps to go,* she thought. *I can't do it. I can't. I can't!*

As the runners neared the end of the track, Olivia slowed down and leaned over, clutching her leg. The other runners pounded ahead.

Mr Roberts ran over to her, looking concerned. "Olivia, what–" he started to say.

Without thinking, Olivia backed away, still grabbing her leg. "I don't know what happened," she moaned. "I think I pulled something."

She limped off the track and towards the school. She was so embarrassed and mad at herself. Worst of all, she knew Aunt Naomi and Mum had seen the whole thing.

Chapter seven

COMING CLEAN

Olivia pushed open the door to the girls' changing room and ran inside. She hated pretending, but she didn't know how to stop. She heard the changing room door open behind her.

"Olivia!" Aunt Naomi called.

All Olivia could think was that she had to keep up the act. She sat down on one of the benches and pretended to massage her leg.

Aunt Naomi sat down next to Olivia. She gave her a stern look. "Olivia," she said. "What are you doing?"

"I thought I pulled something in my leg," Olivia told her aunt, looking down at the floor. "It really hurt."

It was a lie, pure and simple. She felt awful saying it. *If I'd just run the race, it would be over by now,* Olivia thought.

"Olivia, tell me the truth," her aunt said.

Olivia looked up in surprise. She'd expected her aunt to be sympathetic, not upset with her. She opened her mouth but nothing came out.

Aunt Naomi stared at her. "I knew something was going on when you said you'd dropped out of the first race," she said. "Why are you doing this?"

Olivia's cheeks were flaming. She couldn't stand the thought of her aunt being upset with her.

"I – I don't know," she stammered. "I guess I'm afraid of coming in last." She looked down at the toes of her shoes. "I'm afraid of people laughing at me."

Olivia glanced up, expecting her aunt to be angry, but Aunt Naomi looked confused.

"But you've been running for years," her aunt said. "Why would you think you'd come in last? And even if you did, people wouldn't laugh at you. They probably wouldn't even notice."

"I get really nervous before the race," Olivia confessed. "Everyone is watching. I panic. What if I can't keep up? Everyone will laugh at me. I've seen it happen."

Her aunt listened quietly. When Olivia stopped talking, her aunt sighed.

"Olivia, don't you see that you're making more trouble for yourself this way?" Aunt Naomi said. "You don't even know how the races would turn out – maybe you wouldn't come in last at all. And even if you did, it wouldn't be the end of the world. You'd just try to do better in the next race. You can't keep doing this."

Olivia felt horrible. Being lectured by her favourite aunt was as embarrassing as coming in last in a race. But she knew what her aunt was saying was true. "Yeah, I know," she whispered.

Her aunt smiled. "I know you do," she replied. She squeezed Olivia's shoulder and started to lead her from the changing room. "You just need some extra coaching."

They pushed open the door and walked out of the changing room. "When's your next meet?" Aunt Naomi asked.

"In a few days," Olivia replied.

"Perfect," Aunt Naomi said. "We're going to meet back here at the track tonight. And we're going to run the 3200 – at race speed. I'll get today's winning time from your coach. Let's see if we can beat it."

Chapter eight

NO PRESSURE

Later that evening, Olivia paced on the empty track and waited for her aunt to arrive. Every few seconds, she bent over to touch her toes or hopped up and down a few times, trying to stay loose.

Olivia wasn't really sure Aunt Naomi's plan would help. But she didn't have any better ideas.

Anything is better than dropping out of the race, Olivia thought.

Just then, Olivia heard footsteps. She looked up to see her aunt jogging towards her. "Hi," Aunt Naomi said as she slowed to a stop. "Are you ready for this?"

Olivia nodded. "Yep, I already stretched," she said.

Aunt Naomi pressed a button on her watch. "I talked to your coach," she said. "He said the winning time for the 3200 today was eleven minutes, five seconds. Let's try to match that, or at least come close."

"But what about the way I always tense up before the race?" Olivia asked, frowning. "Practising isn't going to help with that."

"Actually, I think it might," her aunt said. "You tense up because you're afraid of coming in last, right?"

"Right," Olivia said.

"So, practising with me could help," Aunt Naomi said. "There won't be any pressure. If you can do it now, you'll know you can do it at the meet. If you can't keep up the pace, then we'll figure out a plan B."

Olivia nodded. Her aunt's plan sounded reasonable. Maybe it would even work.

"Okay," Olivia said. "It's worth a try."

"Ready?" Aunt Naomi asked.

"I guess," Olivia said.

Her aunt pressed the start button on her watch, and the two of them took off down the track. Olivia waited for the tension to come. But it didn't happen.

Maybe it's just because there's no one else around, she thought.

"How does this pace feel so far?" Aunt Naomi asked as they rounded the bend in the track.

Olivia listened to her own steady breathing. Her legs felt strong. "Not bad," she said. First lap completed.

Aunt Naomi glanced at her watch. "Well, this is exactly the winning pace for the last race you ran – or almost ran," she said. "So we know you can do it."

"It feels so different than it did during the race," Olivia said.

Aunt Naomi looked over, running easily. "I think it feels so different because you haven't psyched yourself out," she said. "You've always been able to run this pace. It was your fear that was getting in the way."

"Maybe you're right," Olivia said thoughtfully.

Olivia and Aunt Naomi ran on pace for the rest of the distance. Olivia was so relaxed that she almost forgot to count the laps. She couldn't believe what a difference running with her aunt made. She was actually having fun. And she didn't feel any of the panic she'd felt during the race earlier.

When they reached the finish line, Olivia and Aunt Naomi slowed and came to a stop.

"Whew! That's the winning pace. You did it," Aunt Naomi said, wiping her forehead. "It's been a long time since I've run that distance. Come on, let's walk for a few minutes to cool down."

They walked in silence for a bit, breathing deeply. Finally, Aunt Naomi broke the quiet. "So, how do you feel?" she asked.

"I actually feel okay," Olivia replied as they circled the track. Her muscles felt exercised but not exhausted. And her legs still felt strong. A little bubble of hope began to rise in her chest. "Now if I can just hold on to this feeling at the next meet, I'll be all set."

Chapter nine

GOING THE DISTANCE

Olivia was still feeling good at the meet two days later. Her mum and Aunt Naomi were in the stands once again. But this time, she wasn't worried about disappointing them.

Olivia was sitting on the sidelines stretching with Jessica when her aunt walked over.

"Hey, Liv. How are you feeling?" Aunt Naomi asked.

"I feel pretty good," she told her aunt. "Not nervous at all."

Olivia leaned forwards and touched her toes. She actually felt pretty calm. She just had to keep reminding herself how it had felt to run with her aunt the other night. She knew she could do it.

Jessica looked surprised. "Really?" she asked.

Olivia nodded. "Aunt Naomi helped me practise the other night," she explained. "We ran the winning pace from the last meet together. It felt okay."

"You did great," her aunt agreed. "You can absolutely do this. You might not win, but I can guarantee you won't finish last."

Olivia nodded. Her aunt's faith in her helped.

"Well, I better go find a seat," Aunt Naomi said. "I want to have a good view of my favourite niece finishing her race." She grinned.

"Thanks, Aunt Naomi," Olivia said, smiling back. "I'll see you at the finish line."

As the runners lined up for the 3200-metre race, Olivia realised she was excited for the first time since joining the team. She waited for the awful nervous feeling to rise up, but it didn't come.

Olivia took her place on the track with the other racers. She took a deep breath and cleared her mind.

Crack! The starting gun went off, and the runners immediately jumped off the line. This time, Olivia was right there with them.

The lead runner was setting a fast pace, but Olivia stayed calm. She ran steadily, keeping her arms loose at her sides and focusing on her breathing. *Pace yourself,* she thought.

The runners were approaching the stands now. Olivia was running third in the field of six. The stands flashed past in a blur and then they were gone.

The runners headed into the second lap, and Olivia was still running strong. She knew she was safe. She wasn't going to drop out of this race. Whether she came in first or last or in the middle of the pack didn't matter. She was going to finish the race.

Some of the runners were beginning to tire as they headed into the fourth lap of the race. The girl to Olivia's left was breathing heavily.

With a start, Olivia realised that there were two runners behind her. The race was almost halfway finished, and she was still holding steady. *Wow!* she thought. *I'm doing it! I really am!*

The group rounded the far bend, and the runners sped up, pushing themselves even harder. Olivia ran in the middle of the pack, her legs moving steadily, her arms and heart pumping together.

The pack of runners rounded the first bend again and headed down the far stretch. The girl on Olivia's right started to pull ahead. Four people in front of her now.

Coming out of the second bend, they passed the stands one last time. The home stretch loomed up ahead. Olivia could see the finish line stretched across the track. The runners' feet pounded steadily.

Push it! Olivia thought. Adrenaline surged through her veins. She sped past another runner. The finish line was flying towards her. Olivia dug deep and pushed her legs as fast as they possibly could.

Done! She ran across the finish line and slowed to a stop. Moving off to the side of the track, Olivia bent over and put her hands on her knees to catch her breath.

"Olivia!" Aunt Naomi called. She was leaning over the fence from the stands, with Jessica beside her. Olivia rushed over to hug them both. "You came in third!" Aunt Naomi yelled. "Great work!"

"You were amazing!" Jessica squealed, throwing her arms around her friend.

Olivia grinned. "And I wasn't last," she said.

"You most definitely were not," Aunt Naomi agreed. "I'm really proud of you. You stuck with it and finished the race. And you had some serious speed at the end there!"

Olivia nodded. "Thanks," she said, smiling at her aunt. "But I can't exactly take all of the credit. I think I owe at least a little of that to my favourite aunt."

AUTHOR BIO

Emma Carlson Berne has written more than a dozen books for children and young adults, including teen romance novels, biographies and history books. She lives in Cincinnati, Ohio, USA, with her husband, Aaron, her son, Henry and her dog, Holly.

ILLUSTRATOR BIO

Katie Wood fell in love with drawing when she was very small. Since graduating from Loughborough University School of Art and Design in 2004, she has been living her dream working as a freelance illustrator. From her studio in Leicester, England, she creates bright and lively illustrations for books and magazines all over the world.

GLOSSARY

anxious worried

competition contest of some kind

congratulate to tell someone you are pleased because something good happened to the person or because he or she did something well

courage bravery or fearlessness

embarrassed feeling awkward or uncomfortable

ragged uneven or worn out

sprint very fast race run over a short distance

sympathetic understanding or appreciating someone else's troubles

COMPREHENSION QUESTIONS

1. Do you think Olivia's fear of coming in last was justified? Talk about why or why not.

2. Imagine that you're Mr Roberts. Do you think he knew what Olivia was doing? Talk about how you would have dealt with the situation from his point of view.

3. If you were a runner, would you want to run a sprint or a long distance? Talk about the benefits and difficulties of each.

WRITING PROMPTS

1. Olivia's aunt helps her overcome her fear of placing last. Write about a special relationship you have with your aunt, or another adult in your life.

2. Have you ever come in last in a race? Write about how you felt.

3. Olivia faked an injury to get out of running. Do you think her behaviour was right or wrong? Write about some other ways she could have dealt with her fear.

TIPS AND TRICKS FOR TRAINING

Just like any other sport, running takes practice and training to succeed. Ready to start running? Here are a few tips and tricks you should know ahead of time.

- Be sure to stretch both before and after running to help your muscles warm up and cool down.

- Don't rush through your stretches. Hold each stretch for 15-30 seconds to give your muscles time to relax and warm up.

- Keep a running journal or log to track your runs.

- Make sure to include elements of endurance, speed, rest and cross-training.

- When you first start running, make sure to keep your runs short and slow to avoid injury and soreness. You'll need to build up endurance and stamina.

- Know that it's okay to take breaks while running. Alternating running for a set amount of time and then walking for a set amount of time can actually help build up your endurance.

- Set both short-term goals and long-term goals for running. You won't be running a marathon your first time out, but that doesn't mean you can't train for that.

- Switch up your training plan from time to time to keep from getting bored. This will also help you to continually challenge yourself.

GIRLS

with

GAME

READ MORE
SPORT STORIES

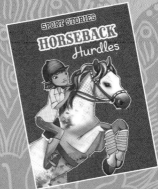

SPORT STORIES

HORSEBACK
Hurdles

SPORT STORIES

Gymnastics
JITTERS

SPORT STORIES

Running
SCARED

SPORT STORIES

Cheer
CHALLENGE

SPORT STORIES

FOOTBALL
SURPRISE

SPORT STORIES

DANCE
DILEMMA